S0-DSZ-232

Belle

The Beast

Lumiere

Starring

Ottoman

Puppy

First published by Parragon in 2010

Parragon
Queen Street House
4 Queen Street
Bath, BA1 1HE, UK

ISBN 978-1-4075-8453-9
Printed in China

Copyright © 2010 Disney Enterprises, Inc.

All rights reserved. No part of this publication may be reproduced, stored in a retrieval system, or transmitted by any means, mechanical, photocopying, recording or otherwise, without the prior permission of the copyright holder.

Belle *and the* Castle Puppy

PaRragon

Bath · New York · Singapore · Hong Kong · Cologne · Delhi · Melbourne

Belle was strolling through the castle garden one chilly
spring day, when she heard a whimpering sound.
A shivering puppy was huddled by the castle gates.
   "Oh, you poor thing!" Belle cried. "Let's get you warmed up
and fed!"
   She cuddled the puppy in her red cloak and hurried to the
castle kitchen.

The enchanted objects laughed when he splashed
in his bath. The dinner forks combed his fur while he
gobbled a bowl of warm stew. Chip and his brothers and
sisters giggled when the puppy drank water from them.
"He's so cute! I hope we can keep him!" Chip said.
But one enchanted object didn't join the fun.

The ottoman watched the puppy. He remembered when he had been a real dog. Suddenly, he wanted some attention, too. With a funny little "grrr," he thumped around the kitchen, trying to act like the puppy. But no one noticed.

Just then, the puppy bounded to the door, barking eagerly.

"Do you want to go out to play?" Belle asked, opening the door.

The poor ottoman wandered off alone while everyone laughed as Belle threw sticks for the puppy to fetch.

Just then, the Beast walked up the path, clutching one of his precious rosebushes.

"Someone has dug up my roses!" he exclaimed.

Then the Beast saw the puppy. "Did that dog dig up my garden? Get rid of him – NOW!"

"I can't leave him in the woods," Belle argued. "He needs a home."

"He's not getting one here!" the Beast roared as he stomped away into the forest. Belle knew that the Beast loved his roses, but what about the puppy?

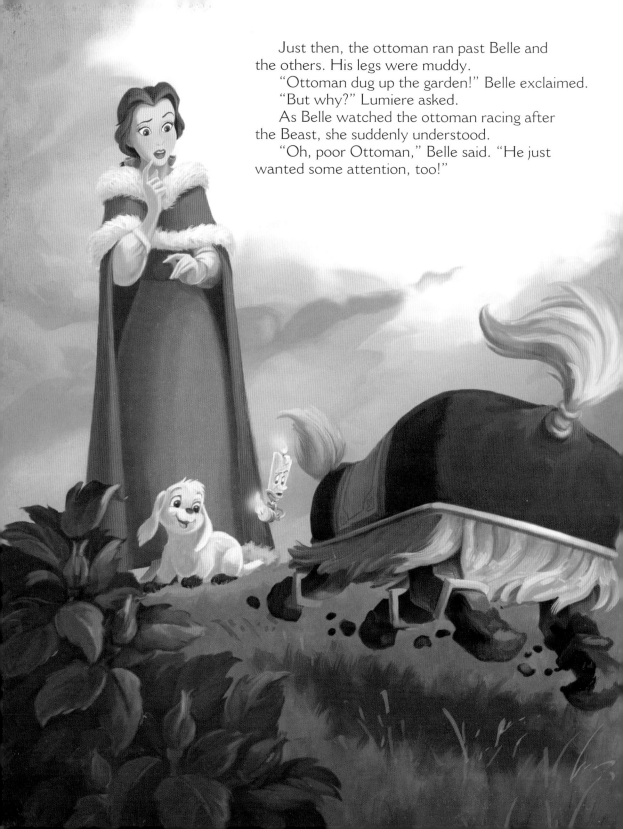

Just then, the ottoman ran past Belle and the others. His legs were muddy.

"Ottoman dug up the garden!" Belle exclaimed.

"But why?" Lumiere asked.

As Belle watched the ottoman racing after the Beast, she suddenly understood.

"Oh, poor Ottoman," Belle said. "He just wanted some attention, too!"

Suddenly, the puppy raced after the ottoman, barking playfully.

Belle tried to call to them, but the ottoman and puppy disappeared among the trees. "They'll get lost!" Belle exclaimed. "I have to bring them back safely."

"But it's getting dark," Mrs Potts protested.

Belle looked at the long shadows creeping through the forest and shivered. Clutching her red cloak tightly, she took a deep breath and started towards the trees.

"Wait!" Lumiere called. "I'll come and light your way."

"Thank you," Belle said as she held Lumiere up high. "I'm glad you're coming."

"Me, too. I think," Lumiere replied. But his flames flickered nervously.

"Puppy! Ottoman!" Belle called as she and Lumiere searched. Something rustled in the bushes. Yellow eyes gleamed at them.

"What is that?" Lumiere whispered.

"I hope it's just squirrels," Belle answered.

"It must be very big squirrels with very big eyes," Lumiere replied.

Belle picked up a large stick. Then she and Lumiere walked on, calling and calling.

Suddenly, they heard ferocious barking and snarling nearby.
Belle ran towards the sound and stumbled into a clearing.
The ottoman and puppy stood below an enormous tree.
Snarling wolves circled them. But the puppy was
growling and snapping back.

"He's protecting Ottoman!" Lumiere
exclaimed.

"He's too small to stop those wolves for
long," Belle answered. "He needs help!"

Quickly, Belle put Lumiere on the ground and lit the stick with his flames. Turning swiftly, Belle ran at the wolves, swinging the blazing stick at them like a flaming sword.

"Get away! Get away!" she shouted.

Snarling angrily, the wolves backed away from the fire. Belle raced between them towards the ottoman and puppy.

But just then Belle tripped on a root.
The torch flew from her hands.
   "Oh, no!" She gasped.
   The torch hit the ground and rolled
just out of her reach. The growling
wolves crept towards her.

Barking fiercely, the puppy raced to the flaming stick. He snatched one end in his teeth and darted among the wolves. As the wolves backed away, the ottoman ran in front of Belle, yapping for her to follow.

"The puppy's clearing the way!" Lumiere shouted to Belle. "Follow Ottoman!"

Suddenly, the Beast crashed into the clearing.
The wolves scattered yelping with fear.

The danger had passed. But the puppy's nose
and ears were singed and sore.

"He and the ottoman tried to save me!" Belle said.

"They are brave little fellows," the Beast answered.
Cradling the puppy in one arm, and the ottoman in the
other, he led Belle to the castle.

When the puppy was cared for, everyone settled by the fireside. Belle watched the Beast stroke the ottoman and feed the puppy biscuits. The gentle smile on his face made her happy.

"May the puppy stay until I can find him a home?" she asked.

The Beast cleared his throat. "His home is here – with us," he answered gruffly. Belle smiled, knowing the Beast loved both of his pets dearly.

The next evening as Belle and the Beast waltzed in the ballroom, the puppy and ottoman kept guard proudly at the door. Both the puppy and the ottoman wore shiny new badges. And on each badge were the words, "Protector of the House."

The End